Anonymous

Report of the Committee of Visitors, of the Bedford Lunatic Asylum

Anatiposi

Anonymous

Report of the Committee of Visitors, of the Bedford Lunatic Asylum

Reprint of the original.

1st Edition 2023　|　ISBN: 978-3-38230-480-5

Anatiposi Verlag is an imprint of Outlook Verlagsgesellschaft mbH.

Verlag (Publisher): Outlook Verlag GmbH, Zeilweg 44, 60439 Frankfurt, Deutschland
Vertretungsberechtigt (Authorized to represent): E. Roepke, Zeilweg 44, 60439 Frankfurt, Deutschland
Druck (Print): Books on Demand GmbH, In de Tarpen 42, 22848 Norderstedt, Deutschland

TABLE VIII.

Form of Insanity.	M.	F.	T.
Mania	3	17	20
Suicidal	3	5	8
with Epilepsy	2	2	4
Suicidal	0	1	1
with General Paralysis	6	2	8
Suicidal	2	0	2
with Delusions	3	16	19
Suicidal	1	2	3
with Hysteria, Suicidal	0	1	1
Melancholia	0	2	2
Suicidal	4	9	13
With Paralysis	0	2	2
Imbecility	3	7	10
Suicidal	2	1	3
with Epilepsy	2	0	2
with Paralysis	0	2	2
with General Paralysis	1	0	1
and Epilepsy	2	0	2
Dementia	0	0	0
Suicidal	1	0	1
with Epilepsy	1	0	1
with General Paralysis	1	0	1
Idiotcy	2	4	6
with Epilepsy	2	0	2
Total	41	73	114

TABLE IX.—STATION OR OCCUPATION.

Males.	No.	Females.	No.
Labourers	24	Servants	9
Groom	1	Lacemakers	3
Mat-maker	1	Plaiters of Straw	5
Straw-cutter	1	Dressmakers	2
Bonnet-presser	1	Bonnet Sewer	5
Journeyman Maltster	1	Sempstresses	3
Engineer Stoker	1	Nurse	1
Cabinet-maker	1	Char-woman	1
Printer	1	Shop-keeper	1
Baker	1	Paper Mill Worker	1
Miller	1	Wives of Labourers	17
Gardener	1	„ Painters	2
Sawyer	1	„ Carpenters	2
Journeyman ironmonger	1	Wife of Bailiff	1
Artilleryman	1	„ Baker	1
No occupation	3	„ Cellar-man	1
		„ Tailor	1
		„ Gardener	1
		Widow of Miller	1
		„ Labourer	1
		„ Farmer	1
		Daughter of Publican	1
		Daughters of Labourers	2
		No occupation	10
Total	41	Total	73

TABLE XVII.

THIS TABLE CONTAINS THE PARTICULARS OF 55 CASES DISCHARGED DURING THE YEAR.

No. on Reg.ster	Age M.	Age F.	Social Condition	No. of Attacks	Occupation	Religion	Mental Disorder	Combinations	Assigned Causes Physical	Assigned Causes Moral	Duration of Disease previous to Admission	Time under Treatment	Cured	Relieved	Recovered by Friends or otherwise
243	25	...	Single	2	Labourer	Baptist	Mania	Epilepsy	Worms		2 years	2 months	...	...	1
227	...	44	Married	...	Wheelwright's wife	Baptist	Melancholia		Critical period	Anxiety of business	10 months	3 months	1		
008	...	44	Ditto	1	House-keeper	Ch.of England	Melancholia		Intemperance, (hereditary)		1 year	3 years	1		
279	...	45	Ditto	2	Baker's wife	Wesleyan	Melancholia	Epilepsy	Epilepsy		8 months	1 month	1		
261	...	27	Ditto	...	Sawyer's wife	Ch.of England	Mania		Puerperal fever		6 months	2 months	1		
232	...	24	Ditto	...	Labourer's wife	Ch.of England	Melancholia		Fever		5 months	5 months	1		
285	...	17	Single	2	Dhtr. of Cellarman	Independent	Mania		Amenorrhœa		1 month	2 months	1		
246	35	...	Married	...	Labourer	Wesleyan	Melancholia		Dyspepsia		1 month	4 months	1		
251	...	66	Ditto	2	Lacemaker	Baptist	Melancholia			Poverty	2 months	5 months	1		
277	...	28	Ditto	2	Rly. labourer's wife	Ch.of England	Mania, delusions		Pregnancy	Jealousy	3 weeks	3 months	1		
069	...	61	Ditto	1	Labourer's wife	Wesleyan	Mania, delusions				5 months	16 months		1	
231	24	...	Single	...	Tailor	Ch.of England	Mania			Domestic trouble	1 week	7 months	1		
245	...	20	Ditto	...	Domestic servant	Ch.of England	Melancholia		Hereditary	Over work	2 weeks	6 months	1		
233	...	45	Married	1	Plaiter	Baptist	Mania		Hereditary	Religious excitmt.	1 week	8 months		1	
236	...	17	Single	...	Servant	Independent	Melancholia		Amenorrhœa	Loss of mother	1 month	8 months	1		
296	...	67	Ditto	2	Dressmaker	Baptist	Mania				2 weeks	4 months	1		
262	67	...	Married	2	Bricklayer	Ch.of England	Imbecility		Intemperance		16 months	6 months	1		
305	...	84	Widow	...	Labourer's wife	Ch.of England	Imbecility				4 weeks	3 months		1	
273	26	...	Married	...	Engineer & stoker	Baptist	Melancholia		Hereditary		8 months	6 months	1		
292	...	45	Ditto	...	Labourer's wife	Baptist	Melancholia			Loss of child	3 weeks	4 months		1	
126	52	...	Ditto	...	Labourer	Ch.of England	Mania, delusions	Paralysis	Disease of brain, intemperance		2 years	2 years		1	
314	...	58	Ditto	...	Labourer's wife	Ch.of England	Melancholia				1 month	3 months	1		
290	...	68	Ditto	...	Carpenter's wife	Baptist	Melancholia	Paralysis			2 months	5 months	1		
318	48	...	Widower	1	Labourer	Ch.of England	Melancholia		Intemperance		3 weeks	2 months	1		
136	78	...	Ditto	1	Labourer	Ch.of England	Imbecility		Injury to head		2 months	2 years	1		
220	...	30	Married	...	Plaiter	Wesleyan	Mania			Illtreat. of husband	2 months	18 months	1		
254	...	68	Widow	1	Labourer's widow	Wesleyan	Imbecility			Religious excitmt.	6 months	7 months		1	
311	...	34	Married	1	Labourer's wife	Ch.of England	Mania				3 weeks	3 months	1		
166	73	...	Widower	...	Engineer & brewer	Wesleyan	Melancholia		Injury to head	Adverse circumst.	9 months	22 months	1		
099	...	26	Married	...	Bonnet sewer	Baptist	Melancholia				3 weeks	10 months	1		
322	...	58	Widow	1	Bonnet sewer	Ch.of England	Mania			Religious excitmut.	3 months	3 months	1		
706	62	...	Married	...	Labourer	Baptist	Mania				7 years				1
222	...	49	Widow	...	Lacemaker	Wesleyan	Mania				1 week	1 year	1		
288	...	38	Married	1	Plaiter	Wesleyan	Melancholia				6 weeks	7 months		1	
960	...	39	Ditto	1	Labourer's wife	Ch.of England	Mania		Hereditary		9 weeks	4 years		1	
325	...	42	Ditto	1	Grocer	Independent	Mania	Paralysis			3 months	3 months	1		
326	19	...	Single	...	Maltster's labourer	Ch.of England	Mania		Injury to the head		1 month	3 months	1		
239	...	38	Married	4	Labourer's wife	Ch.of England	Mania, delusions		Puerperal fever		1 week	11 months	1		
330	...	48	Single	...	Servant	Ch.of England	Mania				2 months	8 months	1		
340	...	26	Ditto	1	Servant	Wesleyan	Mania		Puerperal fever		3 weeks	4 months	1		
002	...	26	Married	...	Dressmaker	Wesleyan	Mania	Hysteria	Puerperal fever		3 months	3 years	1		
389	...	34	Ditto	...		Ch.of England	Mania		Intemperance		2 years	10 years	1		1
313	...	45	Widow	1	Widow of lab.miller	Ch.of England	Mania				8 months	6 months	1		
257	...	34	Married	...	Tailor's wife	Ch.of England	Mania			Jealousy	2 months	11 months		1	
153	49	...	Single	...	Labourer	Ch.of England	Mania					13 years	1		
278	...	51	Married	2	Wife of painter	Ch.of England	Melancholia				3 months	10 months	1		
331	...	25	Ditto	1	Gardener's wife	Ch.of England	Melancholia		Puerperal fever		1 week	5 months	1		
199	23	...	Single	1	Gardener	Ch.of England	Melancholia			Over study	2 months	1½ year	1		
318	...	52	Married	...	Tailor's wife	Ch.of England	Melancholia				2 weeks	4 months	1		
341	...	41	Ditto	1	Labourer's wife	Ch.of England	Mania		Superlactation		1 week	4 months	1		
133	...	55	Single	1	Lacemaker	Baptist	Mania		Hereditary		3 weeks	2½ years		1	
323	...	59	Widow	2	Bonnet sewer	Baptist	Mania		Hereditary		1 year	7 months	1		
356	23	...	Single	...	Jrnyn. ironmonger	Baptist	Mania		Masturbation		1 week	4 months	1		
369	50	...	Married	...	Groom and stable keeper	Ch.of England	Mania	Paralysis		Failure in business	6 months	1 month		1	
353	48	...	Widower	2	Labourer	Ch.of England	Mania		Intemperance		1 week	2 months		1	
	16	39											39	13	3

GENERAL TABLE OF ADMISSIONS,

INCLUDING ALL RE-ADMISSIONS FROM THE OPENING OF THE ASYLUM IN 1812, TO DEC., 31ST, 1858.

	1855.			1856.						1857.						1858.					
	M.	F.	T.	M.	F.	T.	M.	F.	T.	M.	F.	T.	M.	F.	T.	M.	F.	T.	M.	F.	T.
Admissions and Re-admissions	1019	1065	2084	57	54	111	1076	1119	2195	33	56	89	1109	1175	2284	41	73	114	1150	1248	2398
Deduct Re-admissions............	64	80	144	6	9	15	70	89	159	5	12	17	75	101	176	5	18	23	80	119	199
TOTAL	955	985	1940	51	45	96	1006	1030	2036	28	44	72	1034	1074	2108	36	55	91	1070	1129	2199

DIETARY TABLE. No. XVII.

DAYS OF THE WEEK.	BREAKFAST.					DINNER.																SUPPER.								
	Males		Females.			Males.								Females.								Males.					Females.			
	Bread.	Milk Porridge.	Bread.	Butter.	Tea.	Beer.	Bread.	Cooked Meat.	Plum Pudding.	Pie.	Soup.	Stew.	Vegeta-bles.	Beer.	Bread.	Cooked Meat.	Plum Pudding.	Pie.	Soup.	Stew.	Vegeta-bles	Beer.	Bread.	Butter.	Cheese.	Tea.	Bread.	Butter.	Plum Cake.	Tea.
	oz.	pt.	oz.	oz.	pt	pt.	oz.	oz.	oz.	oz.	pt.	pt.	oz.	pt.	oz.	oz.	oz.	oz.	pt.	pt.	oz.	pt.	oz.	oz.	oz.	pt.	oz.	oz.	oz.	pt.
Sunday, ..	7	1½	6	½	1	½	2	6	....	....	....	....	16	½	2	5	...	....	....	....	12	....	7	½	....	1	....	....	8	1
Monday ..	7	1½	6	½	1	....	8	....	....	...	1½	....	....	....	6	....	....	...	1	....	....	½	7	....	1½	....	6	½	...	1
Tuesday ..	7	1½	6	½	1	...	...	6	....	....	...	....	16	....	....	5	....	..	....	..	12	½	7	....	1½	....	6	½	....	1
Wednesday	7	1½	6	½	1	....	6	....	....	....	....	1	....	...	4	....	...	....	....	1	....	½	7	....	½	....	6	½	....	1
Thursday..	7	1½	6	½	1	...	...	6	....	....	...	....	16	...	...	5	....	....	....	....	12	½	7	...	1½	....	6	½	...	1
Friday ...	7	1½	6	½	1	...	....	1½	....	10	....	...	4	...	....	1½	....	10	...	....	4	½	7	....	1½	...	6	½	....	1
Saturday ..	7	1½	6	½	1	...	....	..	16	...	....	....	..	...	....	...	12	....	....	....	....	½	7	....	1½	...	6	½	....	1
TOTALS....	49	10½	42	3½	7	½	16	19½	16	10	1½	1	52	½	12	16½	12	10	1	1	40	3	49	½	9	1	36	3	8	7

N.B.—Scale per Gall. for Porridge....... Twelve ounces Oatmeal, One pint New Milk.
" " Tea. .... One ounce Tea, Four ounces Sugar, One pint New Milk.
" lb. for Plum Pudding.. Eight ounces Flour, One ounce Raisins, and One ounce Treacle.
Soup, for 300 Patients...........The liquor of the Meat the previous day, 75lbs. Legs and Shins of Beef, 14lbs. Peas, 56lbs Carrots, 28lbs. Onions, 14lbs. Oatmeal, Salt, Pepper, Herbs, &c.

Stew for 300 Patients. ....The liquor of the Meat the previous day. 40lbs. Meat, 112lbs Potatoes, 28lbs. Onions, 14lbs. Oatmeal.

EXTRA.—All Male Patients Employed.—Two ounces Bread, ½oz Cheese, and ½-pint Beer at 10 a.m., and ½-pint Beer at 4 p.m.

Women employed at the Wash-house and Laundry.—Six ounces Meat and Vegetables for Dinner on Mondays. Bread and Cheese and ½ pint of Beer at 10 a.m. and at 4 p.m.

Helpers in the Wards and Needlewomen—Bread and Cheese and ½-pint Beer at 10 a.m.

Snuff and Tobacco to be given as indulgences to the workers, &c.

JOHN BARNES, *Steward.*

REPORT

OF THE

COMMITTEE OF VISITORS,

OF THE

Bedford Lunatic Asylum,

FOR THE YEAR ENDING

THE 31st OF DECEMBER, 1858.

WITH APPENDIX.

BEDFORD :

W. C. GREY, PRINTER, AND BOOKSELLER, ST. MARY'S.

MDCCCLIX.

THE COMMITTEE OF VISITORS,

FOR THE YEAR, 1859.

FOR THE COUNTY OF BEDFORD.

THOMAS CHARLES HIGGINS, Esq., Chairman, *Turvey, Newport*
JOHN HARVEY, Esq., *Ickwell Bury, Biggleswade.*   [*Pagnel.*
LIEUT. COLONEL HIGGINS, *Picts Hill, Newport Pagnel.*
HENRY LITTLEDALE, Esq., *Kempston, Bedford.*
CHARLES MOORE, Esq,, *Maulden, Silsoe.*
TALBOT BARNARD, Esq., *Kempston, Bedford.*
WILLIAM LYNN SMART, Esq., *Linden, Woburn.*
MAJOR WILLIAM STUART, *Kempston, Bedford.*
WILLIAM HENRY WHITBREAD, Esq., *Southill, Biggleswade.*
REV. CHAS. COLYEAR BEATY-POWNALL, *Milton Ernest, Bedford.*

FOR THE COUNTY OF HERTFORD.

THE MOST NOBLE THE MARQUIS OF SALISBURY, K. G., *Hatfield.*
RIGHT HON. THE EARL OF VERULAM, *Gorhambury St. Albans.*
THE RIGHT HON. THE LORD DACRE, *The Hoo, Welwyn.*
CAPTAIN WILLIAM FRANKS, 2, *Upper Hyde Park Street,*
THOMAS MILLS, Esq., M.P., *Tolmers, Hertford.*   [*London, W.*
WILLIAM JOHN BLAKE, Esq., *Danesbury, Welwyn.*
GEORGE ROBERT MARTEN, Esq., *Marshalls Wick, Sandridge.*
WILLIAM WILSHERE, Esq., *The Frythe, Welwyn.*
MARLBOROUGH PRYOR, Esq., *Weston, Stevenage.*
REV. FREDERICK SULLIVAN, *Kimpton, Hitchin.*

FOR THE COUNTY OF HUNTINGDON.

COLONEL LINTON, *Stirtloe House, Buckden.*
GEORGE THORNHILL, Esq., *Diddington, Buckden.*
GEORGE WILLIAM ROWLEY, Esq., *The Priory, St. Neots.*
GEORGE RUST, Esq., *Cromwell House, Huntingdon.*
CAPTAIN WILLIAM HUMBLEY, *Eynesbury, St. Neots*
PHILIP TILLARD, Esq., *Stukeley Hall, Huntingdon.*
REV. JAMES LINTON, *Hemingford Abbotts, St. Ives.*

REPORT.

——o——

To Her Majesty's Justices of the Peace for the Counties of Bedford, Hertford, and Huntingdon, in Quarter Sessions assembled.

The Committee of Visitors appointed to superintend the management of the Lunatic Asylum at Bedford, have the honor to report that the arrangements made with the Worcester and Fisherton Asylums for the reception of 30 patients of each sex, referred to in last year's report, have been attended with beneficial results, all applications since made for the admission of patients having been complied with, and consequently new cases have had the great advantage of receiving immediate treatment.

Upon this occasion the Committee have but little to communicate beyond formal matter, owing to the stationary position of the asylum, in anticipation of the opening of the new asylum at Arlsey, in the early part of the year 1860.

The Bedford Asylum has been regularly visited throughout the year. The general state of the health and condition of the patients has been good. One casualty resulting in death, however, has taken place, the particulars of which will be detailed in the Resident Medical Superintendent's report.

The Committee report that the whole of the wooden partitions mentioned in the last annual report have been entirely removed, and iron bedsteads have been substituted. This change has effected a great improvement, and the comfort of the patients has been materially increased.

The Commissioners in Lunacy, on the 14th of June, 1858, made their periodical visit to the Asylum, and entered the following minute in the Visitors' Book, viz. :—

Bedford County Lunatic Asylum, June 14, 1858,

" Since the last visit of the Commissioners on the 6th of August last, 114 patients have been admitted, 83 have been removed or discharged, and 38 have died ; 4 dying from dysentery, 4 from diarrhœa, 7 from paralysis, 5 from diseases of the chest and lungs, and the rest from other causes.

" There are now 299 patients in the Asylum, of whom 141 are males, and 158 females. We understand that 13 are under medical treatment, and that 3 have been secluded during the last week. On reference to the register it appears that there has been no instance of mechanical restraint in the house, but that seclusion has been occasionally resorted to.

" In reference to the points noticed in the last entry, we find that some water-beds and pillows have been procured, and better beds placed in the infirmaries. That the wooden partitions have been removed. That 136 iron bedsteads have been provided, and some small additions made to the stock of washing basins. Some division walls have been removed, and some tweed cloth has been purchased for male clothing ; but as a general dress, the Committee are disposed to continue the grey cloth objected to by the commissioners. A large proportion of the patients, we are informed, take exercise beyond the limits of the premises. Five patients are out on leave ; but we cannot learn that any addition has been made to the 3s. 6d. per week, allowed for the patients' support during absence.

" We think that the yards (which are at present exceedingly bare) would be much improved by placing some cheap climbing plants or creepers against the walls. And we recommend that some additions be made to the stock of cheap secular literature, and that these publications should be distributed amongst the patients of both sexes, and that the attendants be instructed to induce them to read them. Some of the publications (of an amusing sort) might advantageously be read out by the attendants in the evening.

" We are of opinion that the stock of water-jugs and basins for washing should be largely increased ; that these should be placed in the bedrooms, and the patients persuaded, or if necessary, taught to wash and dress themselves. These basins and jugs may safely be transferred to the asylum now in the course of erection, without any danger of conveying there any of the numerous insects which still, we are sorry to learn, infest the present building.

" We do not propose that any outlay should be made in altering the existing asylum, because we trust that the Committee will urge on the completion of the new asylum by every means in their power. We are informed that part of it is already roofed in, and we recommend that such part of it as may now be easily rendered habitable be at once proceeded with, and a portion of the patients removed there, without waiting until the entire asylum can be finished and brought into use for the whole body of patients.

" Amongst the number of patients discharged and removed, we perceive that 30 of the male patients have been removed to the Worcester County Asylum, and 29 females to Fisherton House, near Salisbury. As these patients have thus been placed out of the reach of their friends, we beg to suggest, whether the Committee should not allow to the friends of these patients, the expense of their visiting them in their present residence at all reasonable times.

" We are satisfied that the Bedford Asylum is under very kind and careful superintendance.

B. W. PROCTER, ⎱ Commissioners
S. GASKELL, ⎰ in Lunacy.

With respect to the recommendations of the Commissioners in Lunacy, the Committee refer to their former observations on that head.

The Committee have received a report from Dr. Finch, Medical Proprietor of Fisherton House Asylum, dated December 15, 1858, on the state of the patients sent there from this asylum. He says: " I beg to report for the information of the Committee of Visitors of the lunatic patients of the Bedford Asylum, that the bodily health of these patients has been very good and satisfactory, and that the mental condition of many of them has improved, although I cannot report any one of them sufficiently well to be discharged. No case of injury has occurred, nor have we had any case of death."

The Committee have also been favored with a full report from Dr. Sherlock, Resident Medical Superintendent of the Worcester Asylum, on the state of the patients under his care sent from this asylum. Dr. Sherlock reports that of the 30 male patients suffering from chronic insanity, sent from the Bedford Asylum on the 3rd of November, 1857, 29 still remain under care and treatment; one of them, C. C., a congenital idiot, died on the 10th of August of this year, from exhaustion consequent on diarrhœa. Another patient, J. R., was transferred on the 17th of August following to fill up the vacancy. In general the bodily health of the patients has been remarkably good;

a few of them having suffered from intercurrent disease common to the insane, which though not immediately fatal will probably prove so in time. Almost all the epileptics, of whom there were 9 at the date of their admission, have suffered at intervals from attacks of mania of some severity, and attended in some of the cases with dangerous exhaustion, or from the presence of cerebral congestion of an active form, were in danger of dying during the height of the paroxysms. Several of this class of the patients are in a very advanced form of disease, with little or no power of mind remaining, and are quite unable to assist themselves in the common duties of life. Some of them may be expected to die during the course of any slight illness, or even during a fit. The cases of congenitive idiocy and imbecility have improved considerably in their habits, and their appearance and conduct show less marked indications of this disease. The cases of chronic and recurrent mania continue to suffer from attacks of excitement at irregular intervals, but as a rule these exacerbations are less severe in type and of less frequent occurrence. Several of the cases of advanced dementia have improved very much in their habits, and have become useful and industrious workers, but their improvement has not been carried to such a length as to lead to the impression that they will ultimately recover.

The removal of the epileptics and idiots was attended with a deterioration of their general health for a few weeks, and their habits were more than usually unclean; while the cases of mania were for some time much improved, and only after the lapse of varying periods presented the peculiarities characterising their conduct and excitement. Twenty of the cases are at present in good health and bodily condition; 6 are in moderate health for the most part, but exhibit indications attended with danger to their life at intervals, or have suffered from disease likely to recur; and 4 are in a failing state, and will sooner or later succumb under their malady.

The following table shows the number of patients admitted, discharged, removed, or who have died during the year, viz. :—

ADMISSIONS.	M.	F.	T.
Patients in the Asylum, Dec. 31st, 1857...............	125	142	267
Absent upon trial, Dec. 31st, 1857	0	0	0
Received during the year	41	73	114
Total	166	215	381
DISCHARGES, REMOVALS, AND DEATHS.	M.	F.	T.
Patients discharged—recovered............................	11	28	39
„ „ relieved	3	10	13
„ „ not improved.....................	1	0	1
Removed to other Asylums	1	1	2
Died during the year	10	18	28
Absent upon trial	3	2	5
	29	59	88
Remaining in the Asylum, Dec. 31, 1858	137	156	293
Total	166	215	381

The patients in the Asylum on the 31st of December, 1858, were from the following counties, viz. :—

NAME OF COUNTY, ETC.	M.	F.	T.
Bedfordshire	61	60	121
, Borough of Bedford	2	4	6
Hertfordshire	57	63	120
Huntingdonshire	17	29	46
Total	137	156	293

The patients sent from this Asylum who were confined in Worcester and Fisherton Asylums respectively, on the 31st of December, 1858, were from the following counties, viz. :—

NAME OF COUNTY.	M.	F.	T.
Bedfordshire	11	8	19
Hertfordshire	13	17	30
Huntingdonshire	6	5	11
Total	30	30	60

The daily average number of patients maintained in this Asylum during the year has been 290, or a decrease of 14 compared with last year.

The average number of patients employed during the year has been 186—viz., 80 males and 106 females ; shewing a decrease of 14—viz., 6 males and 8 females, compared with the preceding year.

The average number of patients who attended divine service in chapel during the year has been 89 ; or a decrease of 3 compared with last year.

The deaths during the year have been 28, or a mortality of 7.3 per cent ; the mortality of the year 1857 was 28, showing an increase of 0.3 per cent.

The residue of the statistical information will be published as an appendix to this report.

Lastly, the Committee report that the weekly rate of payment during the year has averaged 9s. 9d. per head per week ; or an increase of 1s. compared with last year. This excess is attributable to the fact that the extra costs incurred in the maintenance of patients in other asylums is charged on the maintenance account of this asylum, and averaged by all the patients of the United Counties accordingly.

Signed on behalf of the Committee,

THO. CHA. HIGGINS, Chairman.

Bedford, December 31st, 1858.

The following Documents are appended to this Report :—

APPENDIX
[A]

REPORT

OF THE

RESIDENT MEDICAL SUPERINTENDENT.

To the Committee of Visitors,
of the Beds., Herts., and Hunts., Lunatic Asylum.

GENTLEMEN,

I have the honor to lay before you my fifth Annual Report of the state of the Asylum, together with the Statistical Tables containing the ages of the patients, their occupation, social condition, religious persuasion, form of disorder, and other particulars connected with the admissions, discharges, and deaths, during the past year, also of those remaining in the Asylum

Although the daily average of patients under treatment has been less by 14, the number of admissions has been larger than on the preceding year, of these 41 were males and 73 females. The form of mental disease being comprised in 66 of mania, 17 melancholia, 20 imbecility, 3 dementia, and 8 idiots. The malady was complicated with paralysis in 16 cases, epilepsy 11, and with a suicidal propensity in 33.

Of the 55 patients discharged, 39 had recovered, 13 were relieved, 1 removed by friends, and 2 transferred to other Asylums, viz., 1 male to the Worcester Asylum, to fill a vacancy caused by the death of an idiot, and 1 in exchange to Fisherton House.

Twenty-eight died during the year, being a fractional increase over the previous one, they were 10 males and 18 females; the causes as will be seen in Table X, were principally paralysis, pulmonary diseases, and exhaustion with general debility.

Three of these call for especial remark, as having been brought to the Asylum in a sinking state, viz., M. F., a female, totally unable to move without assistance, and having a large sore on her back from lying some time in the same position, and neglected as to cleanliness, died on the second day.

W. W., a male, was brought in a carriage, manacled, leg locked, and with a large strap round his body, although he could not stand from extreme exhaustion, died on the fourth day. This case gave ample proof of the benefits of a padded floor, as he did not lie still from that constant rotary motion of the body peculiar to some epileptics, in which a bed would have been unsafe.

The third, a male, J. H., was in a perfect state of inanition from having refused his food for (it is reported) three weeks; the surface of his body was blue, the conjunctiva was injected and arid in appearance, with a viscid discharge from that membrane: he was also stated to have had no relief of bowels for three weeks, this patient sunk on the third day.

The health of the patients throughout the year has been remarkably good, altogether free from epidemic diseases of a fatal character, solitary cases of diarrhœa and dysentery occurred, and with but one exception all recovered.

A peculiar affection shewed itself during the months of January and September, assuming the character of spinal irritation, attacking indiscriminately patients and attendants, to the number of between 40 and 50, and having the appearance of being epidemic, but for which no cause could be assigned. At the onset it commenced in some instances with a slight and transient catarrh, in others, simply tenderness the whole length of two or three of the ribs, with a sensation of constriction of the abdominal muscles ; this led to an examination of the vertebræ, when it was found there was tenderness on pressure in from one to four of the dorsal vertebræ, in no instance above the second or below the sixth ; the remedy used was a strong tincture of iodine painted on each side of the spine, and in no instance did it fail to effect a cure.

The only case on which a Coroner's inquest was held, was on a female who committed suicide by hanging herself. She was admitted in the summer in a state of great excitement, in whose history no mention was made of having a propensity to suicide, yet from the first she firmly resisted her food by clenching her teeth together in a most determined manner ; she was induced to take food in a few days, when it was found there was a large wound on the roof of the mouth, which she stated was done with a spoon whilst feeding her at home ; at the end of six weeks (and during the temporary absence of your Medical Superintendendent) she became violent and was placed in seclusion, when it appears she was impelled by a sudden suicidal paroxysm to suspend herself to the bars of the window by a sheet, and although the means for resuscitation were immediately used, it was without effect.

The medical, combined with the moral treatment of the inmates of this Asylum has been attended with such success in subduing the violent, elevating the melancholic, and raising the feeble to a state of usefulness, as to strengthen your Medical Superintendent in the opinion he has always maintained, of its being the only legitimate system for adoption with the insane ; not that he would make it as a novelty, but simply adding a link to the chain of evidence of those, who so ably advocate that humane view, and by which he is buoyed up with the hope that the time is not far distant, when every convenience may be afforded for carrying it out to its highest advantage.

It is however to be deplored, that in this, as in most County Asylums, the majority is large, of cases in which no prospect of cure can reasonably be expected; as after a careful examination at the end of the year, no more than 9 males and 21 females could be viewed as bearing a chance of recovery. Every attempt has been made to carry out your wishes, coupled with the suggestions of the Commissioners in Lunacy of making trial of those quiet in conduct and cleanly in their habits, of which it is gratifying to state few have returned.

The alterations mentioned in the last report were completed early in the spring, and have been fraught with unbounded satisfaction and comfort to the patients on both sides of the house; the change was effected by the removal of the boarded partitions and fixed cribs, and substituting iron bedsteads, and thus forming four large dormitories, two of 24, and two of 18 beds. It is worthy of remark that a large number of these patients had slept in these small single rooms for years, and although principally of the refractory class, not a casualty has occurred, but now forms a quiet division of the house.

Two patients were received far advanced in pregnancy; the first recovered in time to allow her removal to her family. The second was safely delivered of a fine male child, within these walls, who was so much excited at the sight of her infant, and even intimated a desire to destroy it, that it was deemed advisable to remove it altogether from her, and the father concurring in that opinion, provided a nurse for it, at his house.

Every advantage has been taken, as previously, of affording diversion to the patients, by walks in the country, visits to places of amusement, together with out-door games of cricket and football, and in-doors by fortnightly dances, during the winter months on the female side. On Twelfth night a large Christmas Tree was provided, tastefully decorated with a present for each, at which, with the exception of six in bed, all attended; and notwithstanding the assemblage of all classes, it terminated at a late hour, without one patient either becoming excited or in any way disturbing the merriment of the evening.

It is most gratifying to witness the marked improvement in the conduct of many of the patients, and the devout feeling instilled into them by the additional time and labor kindly bestowed upon them by the Chaplain.

Mention must be made (as illustrative of the contentment of the patients in this Asylum) that not a single escape has taken place during the year.

The Commissioners in Lunacy made their annual visit to the Asylum, and recorded their opinion of the state of the patients and the Asylum.

With renewed thanks for the many kind favors received at your hands,

I have the honor to be,

Gentlemen,

Your obedient and faithful Servant,

WM. DENNE.

APPENDIX
[B]

REPORT OF THE CHAPLAIN.

To the Committee of Visitors of the Bedford Asylum.

GENTLEMEN,

The duties belonging to my office have been discharged by me during the past year to the best of my ability, and with no other interruptions than those occasioned by absences of three weeks in the summer, and a week during the present winter. My place was well supplied at those times by the kind assistance of friends.

The liberal grant of the Visiting Justices has enabled me to provide a library of religious, useful, and entertaining books. The Bible classes have been well attended during the past year, and the number of patients who take a part by reading aloud is on the average about thirteen. Immediately after the reading is concluded commences the reception of books which have been lent, and the distribution of fresh ones. I have preserved an account of our proceedings, which may be summed up as follows:—

Between the 29th of June, the first day of issue of books, and the 19th of January, I have made 245 entries of books lent. They have been eagerly sought after, generally read with interest, well taken care of, and returned with as much regularity as the books of a town and county library. Very few books have been retained so long as to excite a suspicion of their loss; and not more than two or three are, apparently, altogether missing. The library consists of about 50 volumes, and will be considerably increased when the next annual grant is made, to the gratification no doubt of some who have almost made their way through the present list of books. The History of England is sometimes asked for, but well written tales are most in demand. Some confine themselves almost exclusively to religious books, but Robinson Crusoe is attractive even to them. As far as I am able to judge, I think that the attempt to interest and benefit the patients by providing a variety of books, has been most successful.

I have the honor to be,

Gentlemen,

Your obedient Servant,

EDWARD SWANN,

Chaplain.

February 8th, 1859.

APPENDIX
[C]

STATISTICAL TABLES

BY THE

RESIDENT MEDICAL SUPERINTENDENT.

TABLE I.

GENERAL RESULTS OF THE YEAR.

ADMISSIONS, ETC.				M.	F.	T.
Patients in the Asylum, Dec. 31st, 1857				125	142	267
Received during the year				41	73	114
Total under treatment				166	215	381

REMOVED DURING THE YEAR.	M.	F.	T.			
Recovered	11	28	39			
Relieved	3	10	13			
Not improved	1	0	1			
Removed to other Asylums	1	1	2			
	16	39	55			
Died	10	18	28			
Absent upon trial	3	2	5			
	29	59	88			
				29	59	88
Remaining in the Asylum, Dec. 31, 1858				137	156	293

TABLE II.

NUMBER OF ADMISSIONS, DISCHARGES, AND DEATHS, DURING EACH MONTH
IN THE YEAR.

Months.	Admissions.			Discharges.			Deaths.		
	M.	F.	T.	M.	F.	T.	M.	F.	T.
January	7	11	18	1	2	3	1	4	5
February	3	13	16	0	2	2	2	3	5
March	7	3	10	1	2	3	1	1	2
April	3	4	7	0	2	2	2	2	4
May	2	4	6	1	2	3	1	2	3
June	4	10	14	2	5	7	0	1	1
July	5	10	15	3	5	8	0	2	2
August	3	2	5	2	2	4	0	1	1
September	0	5	5	1	6	7	2	0	2
October	2	3	5	1	4	5	0	1	1
November	3	2	5	2	5	7	0	1	1
December	2	6	8	2	2	4	1	0	1
Total	41	73	114	16	39	55	10	18	28

*** *The Seven following Tables contain the particulars of 114 cases
admitted during the year.*

TABLE III.

Age.	M.	F.	T.
From 10 to 20 years	5	3	8
„ 20 to 30 „	13	12	25
„ 30 to 40 „	4	18	22
„ 40 to 50 „	7	13	20
„ 50 to 60 „	5	15	20
„ 60 to 70 „	5	5	10
„ 70 to 80 „	1	4	5
„ 80 to 90 „	0	1	1
Not ascertained	1	2	3
Total	41	73	114

TABLE IV.

Social Condition.	M.	F.	T.
Single	20	28	48
Married	14	32	46
Widowers	7	0	7
Widows	0	11	11
Not ascertained	0	2	2
Total	41	73	114

TABLE V.

Religious Persuasion.	M.	F.	T.
Church of England	30	46	76
Roman Catholic	1	1	2
Wesleyan	3	6	9
Baptist	3	10	13
Independent	0	2	2
Presbyterian	1	0	1
Not ascertained	3	8	11
Total	41	73	114

TABLE VI.

No. of Attacks.	M.	F.	T.
First Attack	27	31	58
Second ditto, or more	6	36	42
Congenital	8	6	14
Total	41	73	114

TABLE VII.

Duration of Disease on Admission.	M.	F.	T.
Not exceeding 1 week	4	8	12
,, ,, 2 ,,	2	5	7
,, ,, 1 month	4	9	13
,, ,, 2 ,,	4	10	14
,, ,, 3 ,,	3	7	10
,, ,, 4 ,,	2	7	9
,, ,, 6 ,,	4	2	6
,, ,, 9 ,,	2	1	3
,, ,, 1 year	1	3	4
,, ,, 2 ,,	3	1	4
,, ,, 3 ,,	0	3	3
,, ,, 4 ,,	1	0	1
,, ,, 5 ,,	0	2	2
,, ,, 6 ,,	1	0	1
,, ,, 8 ,,	0	1	1
,, ,, 14 ,,	1	0	1
,, ,, 15 ,,	1	0	1
,, ,, 17 ,,	1	0	1
,, ,, 56 ,,	0	1	1
From Childhood	1	6	7
Not ascertained	6	7	13
Total	41	73	114

TABLE X.

TABLE OF MORTALITY DURING THE YEAR.

No.	Form of Disease, "Mental."	Age. M.	Age. F	Cause of Death.	Duration of disease (mental.)	Time under treatment.
6	Mania	...	60	Congestion of the lungs, with disease of heart	... ...	23 years
1256	Mania	...	48	Ditto, ditto	4 years...	17 days
1021	Melancholia	...	22	Bronchitis	4 years...	3¼ years
1014	Melancholia	50	...	Pulmonary consumption ...	2½ years	2½ years
1190	Imbecility	...	73	General debility	... ...	9 months
1240	Mania with general Paralysis	58	...	Exhaustion after mania ...	5 months	3 months
1195	Melancholia with Paralysis...	...	52	Paralysis	11 mths.	9 months
1287	Mania	...	53	Exhaustion	9 days ...	2 days
1100	Melancholia	38	...	Exhaustion	3½ years	2 years
1244	Mania	...	24	Exhaustion	3 months	3 months
1295	Dementia with Epilepsy ...	67	...	Exhaustion	2 months	4 days
1211	Melancholia	...	63	Paralysis	8½ mths.	8 months
1095	Idiotcy	22	...	Pulmonary consumption ...	frm birth	2 years
1092	Mania with Delusions	...	84	General debility	3 years...	2 years
1196	Idiotcy	37	...	General debility	frm birth	1 year
1301	Mania with general Paralysis	...	75	General paralysis...	1 year ...	6 weeks
1353	Mania	...	63	Apoplexy	2½ years	2¼ years
1312	Imbecility with Paralysis ...	...	75	Paralysis	1 year ...	5 weeks
1191	Imbecility with Epilepsy......	...	42	Epilepsy...	3¼ years	15 mths.
1208	Mania with general Paralysis	...	47	General paralysis	17 mths.	13 mths.
1327	Mania	...	35	Strangulation inflicted by herself	7 weeks	6 weeks
1226	Melancholia	42	...	Pulmonary consumption ...	3¼ years	8 months
951	Dementia	...	64	Pulmonary consumption ...	5½ years	4 years
1309	Imbecility with gen. Paralysis	48	...	General paralysis...	2 years...	6 months
1171	Imbecility with general Paralysis and Epilepsy	42	...	General paralysis...	2¼ years	1¾ years
1271	Imbecility	...	56	Exhaustion after dysentery	... ...	10 mths.
1346	Imbecility	...	70	Paralysis	1 year ...	5 months
1375	Dementia	62	...	Exhaustion	10 weeks	2 days
	Total...	10	18			

TABLE XI.

STATION OR OCCUPATION.

Males.	No.	Females.	No.
Labourers	4	Wives of Labourers	2
Carpenter	1	Char-women	2
Bricklayer......................	1	Lacemaker	1
Farmer	1	Plaiters	2
Cow-keeper	1	Bonnet Sewer	1
Beer retailer	1	Servant	1
No occupation	1	Sempstress	1
		Nurse	1
		Wife of Painter	1
		„ Blacksmith	1
		Daughters of Labourers ...	2
		No occupation	3
Total	10	Total	18

TABLE XII.

Social Condition.	M.	F.	T.
Married	5	8	13
Widowed	2	4	6
Single	3	6	9
Total	10	18	28

TABLE XIII.

FORM OF DISEASE IN THE CASES OF THE 298 PATIENTS REMAINING IN THE ASYLUM, DECEMBER 31ST, 1858.

Form of Disease.	M.	F.	T.	M.	F.	T.
Mania	21	47	68			
Suicidal	4	3	7			
with Epilepsy	9	2	11			
Suicidal	1	3	4			
with Paralysis	2	2	4			
and Epilepsy	1	0	1			
with General Paralysis	10	1	11			
and Epilepsy	2	0	2			
with Delusions	14	24	38			
Suicidal	2	4	6			
with Hysteria	0	3	3			
Suicidal	0	1	1	66	90	156
Melancholia	8	7	15			
Suicidal	5	11	16			
with Epilepsy Suicidal	1	3	4			
with General Paralysis	1	0	1	15	21	36
Incoherence	1	1	2	1	1	2
Imbecility	22	16	38			
Suicidal	0	2	2			
with Epilepsy	7	5	12			
Suicidal	0	2	2			
with Paralysis	2	1	3			
Senile	0	1	1	31	27	58
Dementia	11	6	17			
with Epilepsy	1	1	2			
with Paralysis	2	0	2	14	7	21
Idiotcy	10	11	21			
with Epilepsy	3	1	4	13	12	25
Total				140	158	298

TABLE XIV.

Age.	M.	F.	T.
From 10 to 20 years	9	5	14
„ 20 to 30 „	29	32	61
„ 30 to 40 „	38	33	71
„ 40 to 50 „	23	28	51
„ 50 to 60 „	21	33	54
„ 60 to 70 „	9	18	27
„ 70 to 80 „	6	7	13
„ 90 to 100 „	0	1	1
Not ascertained	5	1	6
Total	140	158	298

TABLE XV.

Social Condition.	M.	F.	T.
Single	91	98	189
Married	33	35	68
Widowed	14	22	36
Not ascertained	2	3	5
Total	140	158	298

TABLE XVI.

Religious Persuasion.	M.	F.	T.
Church of England	89	102	191
Roman Catholic	1	2	3
Wesleyan	10	10	20
Baptist	7	13	20
Independent	2	5	7
Presbyterian	1	1	2
Not ascertained	30	25	55
Total	140	158	298

TABLE XIX.

ATTENDANTS' AND SERVANTS' RATIONS.

MALES.		FEMALES.	
Weekly.	Daily.	Weekly.	Daily.

4oz. Coffee
½lb. Moist Sugar
¾lb. Cheese
½lb. Butter, or
1lb. Bacon
Fruit and other
  puddings twice.
	1lb. Bread
	1lb. cooked Meat
	3 pints Beer
	¼-pint new milk
	Vegetables accor-
	  ding to season.
		3oz. Tea
		½lb. loaf Sugar,
		or
		¾lb. moist ditto
		½lb. Cheese
		½lb. Butter, or
		1lb. Bacon
		Fruit and other
		  Puddings twice.
			1lb. Bread
			¾lb. cooked meat
			1½-pints Beer
			¼-pint new milk
			Vegetables accor-
			  ding to season.

TABLE XX.

A RETURN OF MATERIALS AND CLOTHING IN STORE DEC. 31ST, 1858.

MATERIAL.		CLOTHING.	
Calico	487yds.	Aprons	109
Corduroy	142 ,,	Bonnets (straw)	57
Cotton Print	170 ,,	Boots and Shoes (pairs)	33
Drabbette	137 ,,	Braces	120
Fustian	59 ,,	Caps (men's)	6
Flannel	100 ,,	Caps (women's)	47
Glazed Lining	159 ,,	Chemises	25
Holland	21 ,,	Drawers	8
Jean	16 ,,	Flannel Shirts	20
Lindsey Wolsey	60 ,,	Flannel Chemises	5
Linen Check	22 ,,	Girls' Frocks	3
Pilot Cloth	36 ,,	Gloves	8
Serge	37 ,,	Handkerchiefs	91
Tweed	16 ,,	Neckerchiefs	27
Leather	159lbs.	Jackets	9
		Waistcoats	25
		Trousers	13
		Night-caps	11
		Night Gowns	5
		Petticoats	135
		Pinafores	4
		Shawls	45
		Shirts	86
		Stays	55
		Stocks	39
		Stockings	275
		Women's Gowns	70

JOHN BARNES, *Steward.*

TABLE XXI.

A RETURN OF CLOTHING AND OTHER ARTICLES MADE AND REPAIRED IN THE
ASYLUM DURING THE YEAR 1858.

MALES.	MADE.	REPD.	FEMALES.	MADE.	REPD.
Bed Ticks..................	5		Aprons	288	512
Boots and Shoes	492	362	Bed Ticks	173	254
Caps	176	75	Blankets..................		82
Coats and Jackets	156	320	Blouses	41	
Waistcoats	128	190	Bonnets (straw).........	53	34
Trousers	124	715	Boots & shoes bd. (prs.)	106	
Leggings	2		Boys' linen Collars......	26	
Flannel Drawers	12		Caps	186	607
Shirts	2		Carpets	12	
Bolsters	12		Chemises..................	395	2943
Hair Mattress	1		Chair Covers	4	
Quilted Rugs	1		Drawers	26	
			Dusters	150	
ATTENDANTS AND SERVANTS.			Frocks....................	51	
			Gowns	323	2581
Coats......................	27	25	Handkerchiefs	438	
Waistcoats	28	18	Holland Jackets.........	32	
Trousers	26	15	Infants' Gowns	29	
			,, Shirts	36	
			,, Caps	4	
			Lace (yards)	84	
			Mattress Cases	4	
			Night Caps..............	50	
			Night Gowns............	50	
			Night Jackets............	20	143
			Petticoats	153	2916
			Pinafores	139	172
			Pillow Ticks	116	68
			Pillow Cases	261	193
			Shirts	536	1075
			Shrouds	13	
			Sheets.....................	145	2946
			,, for Invalid Beds	40	
			Smock Frocks............	18	
			Straw Hats..............	55	
			Straw Plait (score)......	184	
			Table Cloths	31	16
			Tea Cloths	87	
			Towels	74	
			Velvet Stocks............	40	
			Window Blinds.........	10	
			Woollen Rugs	2	163
Total............	1192	1720	Total............	4485	14705

JOHN BARNES, *Steward.*

APPENDIX
[D]
ABSTRACT OF ANNUAL RETURNS,
16 & 17 VICT., Cap. 97, Schedule D.

Name of Union.	In County Asylum.		In Licensed Houses or otherAsylums		With Friends and in Workhouses.		Total of both Sexes	Persons not in confinement.			
								Dangerous to self or others.		Of Dirty Habits.	
	M	F.	M.	F.	M.	F.		M.	F.	M.	F.
Bedfordshire.											
Ampthill	7	10	2	..	8	8	35	..	..	1	..
Bedford	12	22	3	4	9	8	58	..	..	1	..
Biggleswade	17	9	1	3	9	18	57	..	..	..	..
Hitchin, part of	..	..	..	..	..	..	..			..	..
Leighton Buz.,pt. of	5	2	..	..	2	3	12	..	..	..	1
Luton, part of	11	11	3	2	6	7	40	..	..	..	..
Neots St., part of	1	4	1	..	2	4	12	..	..	..	..
Wellingboro,'part of	..	1	..	..	2	1	4	..	..	..	..
Woburn	5	9	1	..	5	5	25	..	..	..	..
Totals	58	68	11	9	43	54	243			2	1
Hertfordshire.											
Albans St.	11	10	1	3	8	25	58	..	..	..	..
Amersham, part of	..	..	..	..	..	..	..	..	..	..	..
Barnet, part of	1	5	1	2	..	1	10	..	..	..	..
Berkhampstead pt.of	1	1	2	..	..	5	9	..	..	..	..
Bishop Stortford ptof	5	3	2	4	7	11	32	..	..	..	..
Buntingford	1	2	1	2	3	6	15	..	..	..	..
Edmonton, part of	2	..	2	4	2	2	12	..	..	..	..
Hatfield	4	9	3	2	2	6	26	..	..	..	..
Hemel Hempstead	1	5	2	..	4	3	15	1	..	..	..
Hertford	5	3	2	1	4	3	18	..	..	..	..
Hitchin, part of	12	8	1	2	15	10	48	..	..	..	..
Luton, part of	..	..	..	..	..	..	..	..	..	..	..
Royston part of	..	1	..	..	4	3	8	..	..	..	..
Ware	6	6	1	3	6	9	31	..	..	1	2
Watford	7	6	1	2	8	12	36	..	..	..	1
Welwyn	1	2	..	1	..	..	4	..	..	..	..
Totals	57	61	19	26	63	96	322	1		1	3
Huntingdonshire.											
Caxton, part of	1	..	..	..	1	..	2	..	..	..	..
Huntingdon	3	11	1	3	3	6	27	..	..	..	1
Ives, St., part of	6	11	2	1	'2	..	22	..	..	..	..
Neots, St., part of	4	4	2	..	4	9	23	..	..	..	..
Oundle part of	..	..	..	..	1	..	1	..	..	..	..
Peterboro,' part of	4	1	2	1	3	4	15	..	..	..	..
Stamford, part of	..	..	..	..	..	..	..	..	..	..	..
Thrapston, part of	..	..	..	..	..	..	.	..	..	..	..
Totals	18	27	7	5	14	19	90				1
Grand Totals	133	156	37	40	120	169	655	1		3	5

APPENDIX
[E]

REPORT

OF THE

COMMITTEE OF VISITORS

UPON THE AUDIT OF ACCOUNTS OF THE

TREASURER AND CLERK TO THE ASYLUM,

PURSUANT TO 16 & 17 VICT., CAP. 97.

COUNTY LUNATIC ASYLUM,
Bedford, February 8th, 1859.

The Committee of Visitors have the honor to report to the Courts of Quarter Sessions of the united Counties of Bedford, Hertford, and Huntingdon, that in pursuance of the Statute 16 & 17 Vict., cap. 97, section LX, they have audited the accounts of the Treasurer and Clerk to the Asylum, at Bedford, and that they have found the same to be correct.

	£	s.	d.
The total Receipts for the year (exclusive of Balances) have been......................................	9418	12	11
The total Payments for the year (exclusive of Balances) have been	9689	1	0
Shewing an excess of Payments over Receipts of	£270	8	1

The Balances due to the Asylum on the 31st of December, 1858, were as follows, viz.—

	£	s.	d.
From Counties and Unions	186	16	9¼
„ Maintenance Account	191	14	0¾
„ County of Bedford, for repairs.......................	38	0	2½
„ Steward	50	0	0
Total......................	£466	11	1

The Balances due from the Asylum on the 31st of December 1858, were as follows, viz: :—

To Counties and Unions	87	11	11
„ Treasurer	378	19	2
Total	£466	11	1

In the Maintenance Account on the 31st of December, 1857, there was a deficient balance of £12 : 14 : 11¾, which has been increased to £191 : 14 : 0¾, during the last year. This may be ascribed to the extra charges debited to this account, on behalf of the patients at Worcester and Fisherton Asylums, as explained in the last year's report, and the too low rate of payment fixed by the Visitors at the earlier portion of the year; this matter however will be shortly set right in the current year.

The Cash Receipts for the Garden and Farm have been	322	1	5
Add—Value of Vegetables and other produce consumed in the asylum during the year	243	6	8
	£565	8	1
The Payments amount to	145	7	5
	£420	0	8
Add—increase of Live and Dead stock compared with the previous year		1	5 10
Net profit on the year	£421	6	6

This statement shews a diminution in the profits of £85 : 3 : 10, compared with the last year, and may be chiefly ascribed to the fall of prices in most of the articles of agricultural produce. Upon the whole, the Committee consider this statement to be satisfactory.

(*Signed*) THO. CHA. HIGGINS, *Chairman*,
WM. LYNN SMART,
W. HUMBLEY,
MARLBOROUGH PRYOR,
W. B. HIGGINS,
CHAS. MOORE,
TALBOT BARNARD,
HENRY LITTLEDALE.

APPENDIX
[F]

RECEIPTS & PAYMENTS

ON ACCOUNT OF THE

BEDFORD LUNATIC ASYLUM,

IN THE YEAR ENDING DECEMBER 31ST, 1858.

RECEIPTS.

FROM SALES	£.	s.	d.	£.	s.	d.
Produce of Garden and Farm.........	322	1	5			
Sundries, old stores, bones, &c.	21	17	4			
Produce of sales of clothing	99	0	2			
				442	18	11

From Unions and Parishes in the United Counties of Beds., Herts., and Hunts., viz. :—

COUNTY OF BEDFORD.

	£.	s.	d.
Ampthill Union	436	7	0
Bedford Union............................	993	1	5
Biggleswade Union	647	14	11
Leighton Buzzard Union	109	4	0
Luton Union	683	13	2
Wellingborough Union	5	5	2
Woburn Union............................	366	16	0

COUNTY OF HERTFORD.

	£.	s.	d.
Alban's St. Union	583	1	1
Barnet Union	149	6	7
Berkhampstead Union...................	101	18	5
Bishop Stortford Union	293	2	5
Buntingford Union	148	13	0
Edmonton Union.........................	70	7	6
Hatfield Union..............	334	8	8
Hemel Hempstead Union	204	16	1

	£.	s.	d.			
Carried forward	£5127	15	5	442	18	11

	£.	s.	d.	£.	s.	d.
Brought forward	5127	15	5	442	18	11
Hertford Union	278	7	6			
Hitchin Union	588	4	9			
Royston Union.....................	50	0	2			
Ware Union........................	377	5	5			
Watford Union	381	14	11			
Welwyn Union.....................	87	1	6			

COUNTY OF HUNTINGDON.

	£.	s.	d.	£.	s.	d.
Caxton Union	24	15	6			
Huntingdon Union	488	18	6			
St. Ives Union	501	7	0			
St. Neots Union	382	12	9			
Peterborough Union	204	7	6			
				8492	10	11

*From the County, Liberty, and Borough Treasurers,
in the United Counties, for Vagrants, Paupers,
& Criminal Lunatics, respectively, viz.:—*

	£.	s.	d.	£.	s.	d.
Albans, St. Liberty	36	8	0			
Bedford, County	160	13	0			
Hertford, County..................	77	14	10			
Huntingdon, County	62	15	10			
				337	11	8

*From the following Counties for the excess in the
weekly sums paid for Criminal Lunatics chargea-
ble to parishes beyond the sums charged for
maintenance of Patients in this Asylum.*— (16 &
17 *Vict., cap* 97, *s.* 42) *viz.:—*

	£.	s.	d.	£.	s.	d.
Bedford County	8	15	6			
Hertford County...................	17	11	0			
				26	6	6

From the County of Bedford.

	£.	s.	d.
For ordinary repairs	119	4	11

	£.	s.	d.
Total Receipts	£9418	12	11

PAYMENTS.

PROVISIONS.	£.	s.	d.	£.	s.	d.
Arrowroot, 74 ℔s. @ 8d. & 10d. ℔ ℔.	2	10	0			
Bacon, 1621 ℔s. @ 7¼d. & 8d. ℔ ℔.	53	11	10			
Baking	10	12	10			
Beer, 17710 gals. @ 7¼ ℔ gal *viz.:*—						
Malt, 1146 bus. at 8s.						
6d. ℔ bus. 487 1 0						
Hops, 1453 ℔s. @ 6¾d. to						
8¼d. ℔ ℔. 45 13 5						
Yeast 0 19 10						
	533	14	3			
Bread, 30424 loaves at 4¼d. & 4¾d.						
℔ loaf	554	0	1			
Buns	2	15	0			
Butter, 4720 ℔s. @ 90s. & 95s. ℔						
cwt., & 1s. to 1s. 3d. ℔ ℔	205	0	9			
Cheese, 7473¾ ℔s. @ 67s. 6d., to						
76s. ℔ cwt	233	4	4			
Coffee, 280 ℔s. @ 1s. 1d. to 1s. 3d.						
℔ ℔	16	6	8			
Currants, 869 ℔s. @ 41s. to 60s. ℔						
cwt.	19	0	6			
Eggs, 160 @ 1s. 8d. & 2s. 1d. ℔ sc.	0	15	5			
Fish	0	5	2			
Flour, 50 sacks @ 31s. to 36s. 6d.						
℔ sack	88	5	0			
Fruit	4	5	0			
Meat, 52589 ℔s. @ 2¼d. to 6d. ℔ ℔.	1196	18	6			
Milk, 3664 gals. @ 7d. ℔ gal.	106	17	4			
Oatmeal, 21¾ sacks @ at 48s. 3d. &						
49s. 3d. ℔ sack	53	8	2			
Peas, 12 bus. @ 7s. 9d. to 8s. 6d. ℔						
bus.	4	19	6			
Poultry	0	6	0			
Raisins, 840 ℔s. @ 42s. to 60s. ℔						
cwt	20	0	4			
Rice, 270 ℔s. @ 18s. to 22s. ℔ cwt	2	9	7			
Sago, 26 ℔s. @ 4d.	0	8	8			

Carried forward £3109 14 11

NOTE.—The cost of the Vegetables consumed from the produce of the Garden and Farm during the year, amounts to £228 : 13 : 8, and has been calculated in the cost per head per week, accordingly.

PROVISIONS, *(continued.)*	£.	s.	d.	£.	s.	d.
Brought forward............	3109	14	11			
Sugar, (loaf) 1134 ℔s. @						
6d. to 6½d. ℣ ℔. 29 11 2						
„ (moist) 4648 ℔s. @						
45s. 6d. to 49s. ℣ cwt. 97 2 7						
	126	13	9			
Tea, 1148 ℔s. @ 3s. 4d. ℣ ℔.	191	6	8			
Treacle, 786 ℔s. @ 2¼d. & 2½d. ℣ ℔.	7	7	0			
Vinegar, mustard, pepper, salt, lard,						
and spices	18	18	7			
Wine	0	8	6			
				*3454	9	5

NECESSARIES.

	£.	s.	d.	£.	s.	d.
Candles, 260 ℔s. @ 6s. to 11s ℣						
dozen ℔s.............	9	14	6			
Coals, 447 tons @ 12s. 11d. to 22s.						
℣ ton	292	15	11			
Gas, 332700 cubic feet @ 6s. 2d. ℣						
thousand feet	102	11	8			
Mortars	1	3	6			
Soap, (hard) 60 cwt. 0 qrs.						
6 ℔s. @ 37s. & 38s. ℣						
cwt. 112 2 0						
„ (soft) 8 firkins @						
25s. & 29s. ℣ firkin... 10 4 0						
	122	6	0			
Soda, 39 cwt. 3 qrs. 14 ℔s. @ 8s. & 8s.						
6d. ℣ cwt.	16	9	6			
Starch and Blue...............	8	5	1			
Wood	4	0	0			
				557	6	2

CLOTHING.

	£.	s.	d.	£.	s.	d.
Braces, gloves, and leggings	6	1	8			
Capes	2	16	3			
Caps and bonnets.......................	1	14	0			
Calico	31	14	5			
Cord	28	6	8			
Flannel	8	16	0			
Handkerchiefs	8	17	0			
Carried forward	88	6	0	4011	15	7

* In calculating the cost per head, per week, £1043 : 16 : 6, for maintenance of household, is deducted from this sum, and added to salaries and wages.

CLOTHING, (continued.)	£.	s.	d.	£.	s.	d.
Brought forward	88	6	0	4011	15	7
Lindsey woolsey	19	0	5			
Linen....................................	56	14	6			
Muslin	6	13	3			
Pilot Cloth	36	13	6			
Pocketting	10	10	8			
Print.......................................	43	16	11			
Shirting cloth	41	2	10			
Shoemaking (without wages).........	106	2	6			
Stays	12	0	0			
Stockings	24	16	0			
Strap locks	6	12	0			
Thread, tape, cotton, buttons, wors-ted, &c....................	41	16	8			
Tweed	16	10	8			
Twill mufflers	3	0	0			
Wrappering	1	15	5			
				515	11	4
SURGERY AND DISPENSARY.						
Drugs	35	14	11			
Surgical instruments	0	12	0			
Wine and spirits	52	6	6			
				88	13	5
SALARIES AND WAGES.						
Visiting Surgeon	85	0	0			
Resident Medical Superintendent £200, Gratuity £50	250	0	0			
Matron......................................	100	0	0			
Clerk £100, Gratuity £50	150	0	0			
Chaplain	80	0	0			
Steward £80, Gratuity £15	95	0	0			
Assistant Matron.........................	26	0	0			
Storeman	30	0	0			
Head Male ward attendant............	33	13	6			
Ten Male ward attendants at from £25 to £30 12s........................	271	18	0			
One Male Night attendant............	30	10	0			
Two Gardeners............................	59	8	0			
Nine Female ward attendants at from £12 to £15	131	15	10			
Supernumerary attendant	9	15	6			
Night Nurse...............................	16	13	0			
Carried forward	1369	13	10	4616	0	4

SALARIES AND WAGES, *(continued.)*	£.	s.	d.	£	s.	d.
Brought forward	1369	13	10	4616	0	4
Superintendent's Servant	9	18	0			
Housemaid	8	19	6			
Cook	17	16	6			
Kitchen maid	2	14	9			
Head Laundress	19	0	0			
Two under Laundresses	27	5	0			
Porter	16	0	0			
Two trades Instructors	65	7	0			
Clothing for male ward attendants...	33	19	2			
Sculleryman	12	8	0			
				1583	1	9

MISCELLANEOUS.

	£	s.	d.			
Baskets and repairing same	7	16	3			
Blacking and black lead	2	2	2			
Books and publications	20	1	2			
Brushes and mops	19	5	2			
Bug destroyer	3	8	0			
Charcoal	12	18	9			
Chimney sweeper......................	0	15	0			
Clock cleaning	0	7	0			
Combs	7	8	0			
Cooperage................................	11	4	3			
Corks	0	14	6			
Earthenware.............................	40	12	4			
Easter Offering.........................	0	10	0			
Glazier	5	9	4			
Hearthstones	2	19	5			
House flannel	14	11	6			
Insurance	14	7	6			
Ironmongery	35	2	7			
Matches	0	17	6			
Music	9	15	8			
Oil........	1	8	0			
Postage and carriage	27	1	0			
Posting bills	0	15	0			
Printing, stationery, and advertisements	116	11	10			
Rates and taxes	28	1	6			
Razors	0	3	9			
Register office for servants	1	6	3			
Recreation for patients	2	12	8			
Removal of patients.....................	4	14	0			
Carried forward	393	0	1	6199	2	1

MISCELLANEOUS, *(continued.)*	£.	s.	d.	£.	s.	d.
Brought forward	393	0	1	6199	2	1
Sand	0	4	3			
Snuff and tobacco.........................	76	14	2			
Spectacles.....................................	1	5	0			
Straw...	51	14	4			
Sundries	3	2	4			
Travelling expenses of officers	2	19	3			
Treasurer's bond	1	15	0			
Washing machine	1	4	0			
Waterproof sheeting	6	12	6			
Waste paper.................................	1	10	0			
				*540	0	11

FUNERAL EXPENSES.

Ordinary repairs, for coffins ....*(a)*	13	0	0

REMOVAL OF PATIENTS.

Expenses of removals ....*(a)*	4	10	3

CONVALESCENT PATIENTS.

Allowance to patients absent on trial...............*(a)*	31	12	3

FURNITURE, BEDDING, FIXTURES, AND FITTINGS.

Bedsteads	103	15	0
Blankets	54	11	7
Cistern	7	7	0
Counterpanes	23	11	8
Matting	17	3	0
Sheeting	38	2	9
Tick	14	14	11
Upholsterer	25	4	6
	284	10	5

Building account, viz :—			
Carpenter 43 1 2			
Bricklayer.........30 5 6			
Ironmonger 32 7 0			
Plumber & glazier 2 7 8			
Smith 27 19 1			
	136	0	5
	420	10	10

Carried forward	£7208	16	4

* In calculating the cost per head, per week, £14 : 13 : 0, for straw consumed from produce of Garden and Farm, has been added to this amount.

(a) These sums have been added to the charges for the maintenance, &c., of the respective patients for whom the expenses were incurred.

	£.	s.	d.	£.	s.	d.
Brought forward				7208	16	4

BUILDING ACCOUNT, ORDINARY REPAIRS.

	£	s	d			
Clifton, T. paint brushes...............	0	8	6			
Francis, S., bricks	3	5	0			
Howard, J., lime	4	2	6			
Kilpin, W. W., ironmonger	14	11	5			
Morton and co., galvanized iron roofing	26	3	6			
Page and Co., ironmongers	11	16	3			
Pain, H., ditto	8	11	2			
Sheppard, Stephen, plumber	11	5	10			
Slater, J., bricklayer	37	17	2			
Steers, W., carpenter	55	5	0			
Steward, sundries as per monthly bills	61	13	4			
Stewardson & Taylor, oil, &c..........	8	7	0			
Whittal & Son, timber...................	9	1	7			
Wing, J. T., cement......................	1	18	6			
	254	6	9			
Less—Funeral expenses transferred 13 0 0						
Furniture, fixtures, and fittings, transferred ... 136 0 5						
	149	0	5			
				105	6	4

MAINTENANCE OF CRIMINAL LUNATICS.

				£	s	d
Dr. Finch, for maintenance of patients, from December 21st, 1857, to December 21st, 1858				312	8	0

MAINTENANCE OF PAUPER PATIENTS IN OTHER ASYLUMS.

	£	s	d	£	s	d
Dr. Finch, for maintenance of female patients to 31st December 1858, at 13s. per week 1017 4 2						
Committee of Visitors of Worcester Asylum, for maintenance of male patients to ditto, at 11s. 6d. per wk. 899 18 9						
				1917	2	11

GARDEN AND FARM.

				£	s	d
Orders on Treasurer at various times during the year				145	7	5
Total Payments..............£9689				9689	1	0

THE RATES OF PAYMENT DURING THE YEAR HAVE BEEN AS FOLLOWS, *viz.*—

	£.	s.	d.
First Quarter......	0	9	0
Second Quarter	0	9	6
Third Quarter	0	9	6
Fourth Quarter	0	10	0
	1	18	0
Average	0	9	6

THE ACTUAL WEEKLY COST OF THE PATIENTS AVERAGES AS FOLLOWS, *viz.*:—

	s.	d.	£.	s.	d.
Provisions	3	6			
Necessaries...	0	8¾			
Clothing	0	8¼			
Salaries and Wages	3	5¾			
Surgery and Dispensary	0	1¼			
Fittings and Furniture	0	6¾			
Other expenses	1	5			
			0	10	5¾
Less from miscellaneous receipts......			0	0	10¾
Net cost			0	9	7
Average weekly cost of Household ...			0	9	11¾

Daily average of patients in this Asylum	290
Ditto in Worcester and Fisherton Asylums......	60
Daily average of Household	40

STATEMENT of the RECEIPTS & PAYMENTS

Between the 1st of January

RECEIPTS.

	£	s.	d.
To Balance in Steward's hands 31st Dec., 1858	50	0	0
Receipts under the following heads, *viz.* :—			
PAGE.			
39 Sales—Produce of Garden, Farm, Sundries and Clothing	442	18	11
39 Unions and Parishes in the united Counties of Bedford, Hertford, and Huntingdon ...	8492	10	11
40 County and Borough Treasurers in united Counties	337	11	8
40 Counties of Bedford and Hertford, excess paid for maintenance of criminal lunatics chargeable to parishes (16 & 17 Vict., c. 97, s. 42)	26	6	6
40 County of Bedford, for ordinary repairs	119	4	11
	9468	12	11
Balance due to Treasurer, 31st Dec., 1858	378	19	2
	£9847	12	1

SAMUEL WING,

Clerk to the Committee of Visitors.

ON ACCOUNT OF THE BEDFORD LUNATIC ASYLUM,

and the 31st of December, 1858.

PAYMENTS.

		£.	s.	d.
By Balance due to Treasurer, 31st Dec., 1857...		108	11	1

Payments under the following heads, *viz. :—*

PAGE.		£.	s.	d.			
41	Provisions	3454	9	5			
42	Necessaries	557	6	2			
42	Clothing	515	11	4			
43	Surgery and Dispensary	88	13	5			
43	Salaries and wages	1583	1	9			
44	Miscellaneous	540	0	11			
45	Funerals	13	0	0			
45	Removal of Patients	4	10	3			
45	Allowance to Convalescent Patients	31	12	3			
45	Furniture, Bedding, Fixtures and Fittings	420	10	10			
45	Building Account — Ordinary Repairs	105	6	4			
46	Maintenance of criminal lunatics	312	8	0			
46	Maintenance of Patients in other Asylums	1917	2	11			
46	Garden and Farm	145	7	5			
					9689	1	0
Balance in Steward's hands, 31st Dec., 1858 ..					50	0	0
					£9847	12	1

8th February, 1859, *examined and allowed*,

THO. CHA. HIGGINS,

Chairman.

ABSTRACT of the RECEIPTS & PAYMENTS

For the year ending

RECEIPTS.

			£.	s.	d.	£.	s.	d.
To Cash for sale of Pigs			126	17	4			
,,	,,	Sheep and Lambs	22	6	0			
,,	,,	Wool	3	4	0			
,,	,,	Potatoes	36	15	3			
,,	,,	Onions	71	13	9			
,,	,,	Wheat	30	0	10			
,,	,,	Mangel Wurzel	3	6	3			
,,	,,	Tares	9	0	0			
,,	,,	Cabbages	2	17	0			
,,	,,	Brocoli	1	14	2			
,,	,,	Savoys	6	0	0			
,,	,,	Parsnips	6	0	0			
,,	,,	Poultry............	0	8	0			
,,	,,	Eggs...............	0	2	0			
,,	,,	Green Peas	0	2	6			
,,	,,	Chaff	0	5	0			
,,	,,	Seeds (various)	1	9	4			
						322	1	5
Orders on Treasurer at various times during the year						145	7	5
Provision Account, value of Vegetables consumed in the Asylum during the year						228	13	8
Miscellaneous Account.—Value of Straw						14	13	0
Estimated Rent of old Garden						6	0	0
Value of Grains, Wash, and Straw, consumed on the Garden and Farm during the year						57	11	6
						£774	7	0

SAMUEL WING,

Clerk to the Committee of Visitors.

ON ACCOUNT OF THE GARDEN AND FARM,

and the 31st of December, 1858.

PAYMENTS.

	£.	s.	d.	£.	s.	d.
By Cash for Rent and Taxes	77	19	0			
,, ,, Pigs	1	0	4			
,, ,, Garden Seeds	2	9	8			
,, ,, Pollard	20	12	2			
,, ,, Ironmongery	5	6	0			
,, ,, Rope	0	15	4			
,, ,, Sheep	21	16	2			
,, ,, Tares	4	4	0			
,, ,, Wheat	1	16	0			
,, ,, Thrashing wheat	2	12	0			
,, ,, Hurdles	6	3	0			
,, ,, Sundries	0	13	9			
				145	7	5
Cash to Treasurer at various times during the year				322	1	5
Maintenance Account, value of Vegetables consumed in the Asylum during the year				228	13	8
Straw consumed				14	13	0
Garden Account, estimated Rent, and value of Grains, consumed on the Garden and Farm during the year				63	11	6
				£774	7	0

8th February, 1859, *examined and allowed*,

THO. CHA. HIGGINS,

Chairman.

STATEMENT OF THE VALUE OF LIVE AND DEAD STOCK,

On the 31st December, 1857, and 1858, respectively.

1857.		£.	s.	d.
Dec. 31. Estimated value of live and dead stock, as per last year's account		332	14	6
Increase 1858, compared with 1857		1	5	10
		£334	**0**	**4**

1858.		£.	s.	d.
Dec. 31. Estimated value of live and dead stock this day, *viz :—*				
Growing crops		90	16	4
Manure		25	0	0
Pigs		42	10	0
Poultry		10	19	0
Produce of store		106	12	0
Sheep		58	3	0
		£334	**0**	**4**

8th February, 1859, *examined and allowed,*

THO. CHA. HIGGINS,

Chairman.

SAMUEL WING,

Clerk to the Committee of Visitors.

Annual Abstract

[MAINTENANCE, ETC., ACCOUNT]

Of the Receipts and Expenditure of the Bedford Lunatic Asylum, and of the Balances for the Year ending December 31st, 1858.

NAMES of COUNTIES, &c., AND UNIONS	No. of Collective Days Patients have been in Asylum	RECEIPTS — Balances due to Counties, &c. and Unions last Year (£ s. d.)	Amounts received this Year (£ s. d.)	Total Receipts (£ s. d.)	EXPENDITURE — Proportions of Maintenance, &c. (£ s. d.)	Proportions of other Expenses (£ s. d.)	TOTALS (£ s. d.)	Balance due from Counties, &c. and Unions last Year (£ s. d.)	GRAND TOTALS (£ s. d.)	BALANCES — Balances due to Counties &c. and Unions this Year (£ s. d.)	Balances due from Counties, &c. and Unions this Year (£ s. d.)
Albans St. Liberty	8933	0 1 10	36 8 0	36 9 10	36 8 0		36 8 0		36 8 0	0 1 10	
Albans St. Union	6503	7 1 3	583 1 1	583 1 1	610 18 7	28 10 9	639 9 4	9 2 4	648 11 8		65 10 7
Ampthill Union	2269		443 8 3	443 8 3	441 19 1	3 0 6	444 19 ...		444 8 2		0 19 9
Barnet Union	950	1 1 9	149 6 7	149 6 7	154 19 1	1 0 0	155 19 1	0 3 6	156 8 7		6 16 0
Bedford County	14541	7 12 8	169 1 5	170 10 3	64 16 3	105 14 ...	170 10 3		170 10 3		
Bedford Union	1680	9 0 9	993 1 ...	1000 14 ...	983 0 ...	3 3 6	991 4 ...		991 4 ...	9 10 0	
Berkhampstead Union	10026	40 0 2	101 18 5	110 19 2	114 3 8	0 13 0	114 16 8		114 16 8		3 17 6
Biggleswade Union	4503	14 0 11	647 14 11	687 15 1	681 17 1	28 9 3	710 6 4		710 6 4		22 11 3
Bishop Stortford Union	21190	4 16 2	293 2 5	307 3 4	305 14 10	1 8 6	307 3 4		307 3 4	4 16 2	
Buntingford Union	366	1 4 5	148 13 6	153 9 2	148 15 6		148 13 0		148 13 0	1 4 5	
Caxton Union	1095		24 15 6	26 19 11	24 15 6		24 15 6		24 15 6		
Edmonton Union	4996	0 19 6	70 7 6	70 7 6	74 6 6	1 3	74 6 6	15 15 6	90 2 ...	4 16 2	19 14 6
Hatfield Union	3046		334 8 8	335 8 2	339 12 10	4 19 5	340 14 1		340 14 1	1 4 5	5 5 11
Hemel Hempstead Union	301	0 2 6	204 16 1	204 16 1	206 5 3	55 19 ...	211 4 8	6 18 8	218 3 4		13 7 3
Hertford County	4057	10 16 3	95 5 10	95 8 4	20 13 4	0 13 0	80 9 4		80 9 4	14 19 0	
Hertford Union	8466		278 7 6	289 3 9	275 4 ...	5 14 4	275 17 9		275 17 9	13 6 0	
Hitchin Union	380		588 4 9	588 4 9	574 1 ...	37 1 6	579 15 9	6 13 0	586 8 9		
Huntingdon County	7040	2 11	62 15 10	62 15 10	25 14 10		62 15 10		62 15 10	1 16 0	
Huntingdon Union	7360	2 8 0	488 18 6	491 9 9	477 10 3	0 13 0	478 16 3		478 16 3	12 13 6	
Ives St. Union	2247	3 6 8	501 7 9	503 15 6	499 18 9	6 6 0	500 1 9		500 1 9	3 18 3	
Leighton Buzzard Union	16097	7 9 5½	109 4 6	112 10 8	152 12 9	2 13 0	152 19 9		152 19 9		40 9 1
Luton Union	5392	1 9 0	683 13 2	691 2 7½	685 13 11	0 7 0	691 12 4	4 0 2	691 12 4	10 5 8	0 9 8½
Neots St. Union	3203	0 7 6	382 12 9	382 12 9	365 13 11	2 13 0	368 6 11		372 7 1	0 6 4	
Peterborough Union	722		204 7 6	205 16 6	205 3 2	0 7 0	205 10 2	0 9 2	205 10 2	0 4 6	
Royston Union	4956	0 0 9	50 0 2	50 0 2	48 19 6	0 7 0	49 6 6		49 15 8	10 17 0	
Ware Union	38	0 7 6	377 5 5	377 12 11	337 14 5	29 11 6	366 15 11	6 2 1	366 16 11	2 1 11	
Watford Union	5584		381 14 11	381 14 11	379 14 9	3 13 ...	383 8 ...		389 10 ...	0 13 8	7 16 3
Wellingborough Union	38	0 0 9	5 5 ...	5 5 11	2 11 0	0 13 0	3 4 0		3 4 0		
Welwyn Union	1284	1 1 10	87 1 6	88 3 4	87 9 8		87 9 8		87 9 8	1 2 8	
Woburn Union	6310		366 16 0	366 16 0	359 15 6	4 1 6	363 17 0	1 16 4	365 13 ...		
Totals	**127414**	**115 12 7¼**	**8856 9 1**	**8972 1 8¼**	**8652 9 0**	**367 16 10**	**9020 5 10**	**61 0 9**	**9071 6 7**	**87 11 11**	**186 16 9½**
Compared with last year { Increase	13541		284 0 0	316 7 2		43 16 6					
Decrease }		32 7 2			535 1 7		578 18 1	98 14 2	480 3 11	28 0 8½	135 16 9½

Comparative Table shewing the total Annual Receipts and Expenditure under separate headings, from the year 1849, to 1858, both inclusive.

[Ordered August Quarterly Meeting, 1852.]

Years ending Dec. 31	RECEIPTS			EXPENDITURE									Daily Average number of Patients	Average Weekly Rate of Payment for maintenance of Patients
	Maintenance, &c. of Patients.	From all other Sources.	TOTAL RECEIPTS.	Provisions.	Necessaries.	Clothing.	Surgery and Dispensary.	Salaries and Wages.	Furniture and Bedding.	Building and Repairs.	All other Payments.	TOTAL EXPENDITURE.		
	£ s. d.	£ s. d.	£ s. d.	£ s. d.	£ s. d.	£ s. d.	£ s. d.	£ s. d.	£ s. d.	£ s. d.	£ s. d.	£ s. d.		s. d.
1849	4896 16 10	1427 14 4	6324 11 3	2199 9 0	470 2 9	483 5 11	71 16 1	879 0 9	124 16 3	1952 10 7	512 19 7	7694 0 11	251	7 6
1850	4922 11 4	78 4 5	5000 15 9	2120 15 10	445 7 10	444 1 11	62 0 7	914 14 1	124 3 3	363 15 5	527 5 5	6011 4 6	258	7 3
1851	4752 10 1	931 15 4	5684 5 5	2318 12 7	507 12 9	487 5 3	58 16 8	926 6 11	125 11 10	1193 8 11	728 1	6340 16 0	267	6 9
1852	5357 2 3	463 1 1	5820 4	2375 16 0	518 2 7	512 2 2	35 0 3	993 17 8	303 5 7	307 1 5	599 13	5644 19 1	275	7 4½
1853	5700 19 4	476 0	6176 19 4	2858 0 6	558 19 10	500 3 1	47 19	1007 13 10	164 18 11	301 15 8	783 6	5622 17 9	271	7 10¾
1854	7634 10 11	523 6	8157 16 11	3566 14 1½	611 19 3	760 12 3	51 6	1086 9 0	387 3 6	357 9 10½	1290 4	2813 18 7	284	9 9
1855	8059 5 9	660 8	8719 14 4	4086 15 0	607 13 4	638 4 3	62 15	1432 6 11	614 13 7	217 8	1176 8	10836 6 5	293	10 0
1856	8245 4 1	743 2	8988 6 1	4282 12 2	571 6 11	498 18 9	76 14	1367 19 0	354 3 10	169 13 6	973 2	8294 10 6	307	10 0
1857	7572 9 1	566 12 10	8139 1 11	3881 9 1	549 16 6	563 16 10	83 10 3	1521 5 6	347 2 2	135 4 10	1308 2	9390 7 11	312	8 9
1858	8075 14 0	442 18 11	9418 12 11	3454 9 5	557 6 2	515 11 4	88 13 5	1583 1 9	420 10 10	105 6	2964 1	9659 1 0	350	9 6

CONTENTS.